Misty
to the
Rescue

Other titles in this series

Misty
to the
Rescue

gillian shields

illustrated by helen Turner

BLOOMSBURY
CHILDREN'S
BOOKS

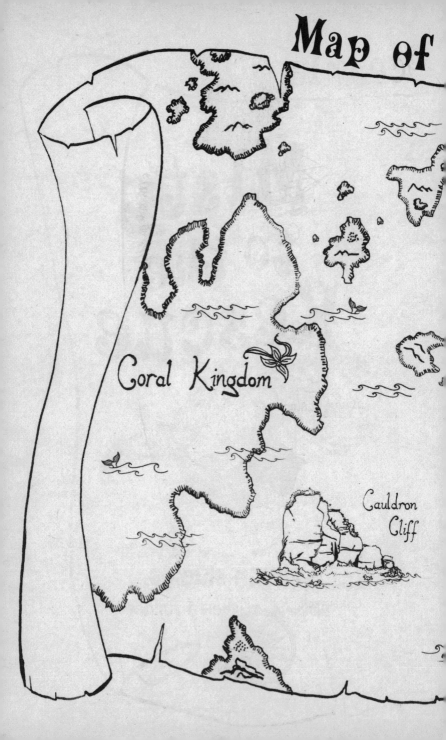

Oceania

Giant Kelp
Forest

Rocky Islands

Fishing
Nets

Shipwreck

N
E
W
S

First published in Great Britain in 2006 by Bloomsbury Publishing Plc,
36 Soho Square, London, W1D 3QY

A CIP catalogue record of this book is available from the British Library

ISBN 978 0 7475 8765 1

Printed and bound in Great Britain by Clays Ltd, St Ives Plc

3 5 7 9 10 8 6 4

All papers used by Bloomsbury Publishing are natural, recyclable products
made from wood grown in well-managed forests. The manufacturing processes
conform to the environmental regulations of the country of origin.

For Daniella

− *G.S.*

For Tom, who always puts
a smile on my face!

Love − H.T.

Prologue

Meet Misty, Ellie, Sophie, Holly,
Lucy and Scarlett. They are mermaid
Sisters of the Sea, who live in the
magical underwater world of Coral
Kingdom. The Merfolk and their
wise ruler, Queen Neptuna, look
after the sea and all its creatures.

Coral Kingdom is protected by six
powerful magic Crystals, which give
life and strength to the Merfolk.

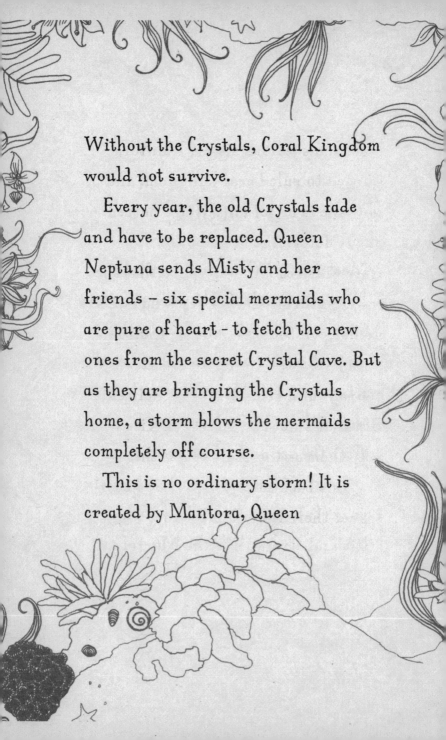

Without the Crystals, Coral Kingdom would not survive.

Every year, the old Crystals fade and have to be replaced. Queen Neptuna sends Misty and her friends – six special mermaids who are pure of heart - to fetch the new ones from the secret Crystal Cave. But as they are bringing the Crystals home, a storm blows the mermaids completely off course.

This is no ordinary storm! It is created by Mantora, Queen

Neptuna's jealous sister. Mantora wanted to rule Coral Kingdom, and now she is bitter and full of hatred. She is determined to stop the mermaids reaching home, so that she can overthrow Queen Neptuna and set up her evil Storm Kingdom instead.

Luckily, the young mermaids have courage and friendship on their side. But that's not all; their SOS Kits will help them as they race to get the Crystals back safely. And they never forget their Mermaid Pledge:

We promise that we'll take good care
Of all sea creatures everywhere.
We'll never hurt and never break,
We'll always give and never take.
And as we fight Mantora's threat,
This saying we must not forget:
'I'll help you and you'll help me,
For we are Sisters Of the Sea!'

Misty and her friends are eager to prove that Queen Neptuna was right to trust them with the precious Crystals. They are going to do everything it takes to get them home and safeguard Coral Kingdom for another year.

Will Mantora win? Or can the mermaids get the new Crystals back in time to stop the light fading for ever from Coral Kingdom?

Misty

Chapter One

'We're here!' said Misty eagerly. 'We're at the Crystal Cave at last.'

Misty, Ellie, Sophie, Holly, Lucy and Scarlett swam slowly into the secret underwater cave that was hidden away on the borders of Coral Kingdom. Misty and her friends had come to the Crystal Cave on a special mission. They were the brightest and bravest young mermaids in the whole of Queen Neptuna's kingdom, and she had taken them aside to give them a very important task.

'Every year the six Crystals in my Throne fade and grow old,' the Queen had told them. 'When they fade, our magical Merfolk power fades too. In one week, these Crystals that you see will be no more.'

The Throne was beautiful. It was at the heart of Coral Kingdom, made of shining silver and inlaid with pearls. At the top of the Throne six magic Crystals glowed around the Queen's head like stars. But the mermaids had noticed that the Crystals were starting to fade. They flickered red and yellow and blue, like candle flames ready to be blown out.

'We need six new Crystals, full of young strength and life, just like you are,' Queen Neptuna had explained. 'Take this key, and go to the Crystal Cave to fetch them. They will protect Coral Kingdom for another year. I trust you with this task, my brave young Sisters of the Sea!'

The friends had felt proud and excited as they set off. Misty guarded the golden key in the little pink pouch of her SOS kit, which was tied round her waist. They had to get the new Crystals home as quickly as possible. Misty and her friends were so honoured that Queen Neptuna had chosen them especially to do this, and they didn't want to let her down, or their families, or the rest of the Merfolk.

The young mermaids had swum for a whole day to reach the Crystal Cave. Misty had been singing happily along the way, but as she led the others into the Underwater cavern, they all fell silent. They had arrived at last. Above the sea, the sun was beginning to set in a rosy cloud. Under the waves, the mermaids gazed in wonder at the cave's golden, glittering walls.

'Look!' said Misty. There was a small silver door set in the wall of the cave. Misty swam towards it, gently swishing her pink tail. Then she took Queen Neptuna's key from her pouch and fitted it into the keyhole, turning it slowly before opening the door.

'Oh!' gasped the mermaids, as they gathered together and watched in amazement.

Behind the door was a tiny chamber. It

was no bigger than a cupboard and lined with mother-of-pearl. In the middle of the chamber were six dazzling Crystals, set out in a gleaming row.

'I have never seen anything so beautiful,' breathed Misty. The Crystals shone brightly, glinting with a hundred coloured sparks of light. They seemed to glow with magical power.

'Aren't they wonderful?' exclaimed Ellie. 'And it has taken them a whole year to grow. We must look after them very carefully.'

'Six Crystals for the Six Folk of the Sea,' murmured Lucy dreamily. 'They really are magical.'

'We'll choose one each,' said Misty, as she turned to the others. 'Then let's try to

sleep. It's almost night-time. We can head for home as soon as the sun rises.'

'We must wake up early,' said Holly in a businesslike voice. 'It's very important to get the new Crystals home before the old ones fade away at the end of the week.'

'But it only took us a day to get here,' said Scarlett. She was arranging her hair, peeping into a little mirror that she had taken from her sparkly red pouch. 'We've got six whole days to get back.'

'I still don't think we should stay here too long,' replied Misty firmly. 'It's a big responsibility to be the Crystal Keepers on our journey home. But if we get back nice and quickly, maybe the Queen will trust us with other tasks.'

'You're right,' agreed Ellie. 'We mustn't risk being late.'

'And if the new Crystals aren't set in Queen Neptuna's Throne before the old ones have faded, the power of the Merfolk will fade too. Then it will be impossible to protect the sea and our kingdom from harm,' said Misty, in a serious voice.

'That would be dreadful,' shuddered Lucy.

'Let's get on with it then,' said Sophie cheerfully. 'You pick the first one, Misty.'

But before she could, Scarlett pushed in.

'*I* want to be first,' she said bossily.

'Honestly, Scarlett,' said Sophie, 'does it

matter who goes first?'

Scarlett ignored Sophie and sulkily tossed her long dark hair over her shoulders. With a flick of her sparkling red tail and a swirl of pearly bubbles, she hovered in front of the secret chamber. She quickly picked up the Crystal that was nearest to her.

'Queen Neptuna said that the first Crystal is to protect the Fish and the Sea Creatures,' Scarlett said. 'I want to choose that one.' Then she tucked it away in her crimson pouch. One by one, the other mermaids did the same. As they picked them up, the Crystals felt full of power and energy. Their magic was very strong.

'I choose the second Crystal to protect the Whales and Dolphins,' said Sophie. She put it in her orange pouch, which matched her bright tail.

'I choose the

third Crystal to protect the Sea Birds,' said Ellie, hiding it in her purple pouch.

'I choose the fourth Crystal to protect the Sea Plants,' said Holly. Away it went into her yellow pouch.

'I choose the fifth Crystal to protect the Merfolk who care for them all,' said Misty. She admired its sparkling colours before putting it away carefully.

There was only one Crystal left.

'And I choose the sixth Crystal to protect the Humans who come to the sea,' said Lucy softly.

'Who wants to protect the Humans?' muttered Sophie. 'Aren't they always causing trouble?'

'The Humans are part of Mother Nature's world too, Sophie,' Lucy said

quietly. She gently placed the sixth Crystal
in her pale green pouch. As she did so, a
rainbow of light poured out of the tiny
chamber. Then the door swung to, and
was sealed by magic. Misty carefully put
the golden key into her pink pouch, next
to her Crystal.

'There!' she said solemnly. 'We
are now the Crystal Keepers.
It's up to us to get them home
safely.'

But just then, a terrible thing
happened.

The mermaids heard the sound of horrible, menacing laughter behind them at the entrance of the cave. A cruel voice called out, 'Powers of the Dark Storm, arise now for me!'

'Oh no,' gasped Misty. 'It's Mantora!'

The mermaids were suddenly thrown into a swirling whirlpool. It sucked them up out of the Crystal Cave and into the open sea.

'Be careful, everyone,' Holly cried out. 'Keep hold of your Crystals!'

'And let's stay together,' called Misty

urgently. She tried to catch hold of Ellie and Lucy's hands. But it was too late! Misty was slipping away from her friends, as the whirlpool turned into a twisting storm. She heard Scarlett scream. Then Misty was lifted right out of the water and hurled through a dark and cloudy sky. The glowing sunset had been transformed into an angry blaze of red, burning like a fierce fire over the sea.

Misty seemed to be blown away for miles, far across the wide ocean, all through the black night. The force of the wind was too strong for her to fight it. But where was she going? And when would it end?

Chapter Two

At last, the unnatural storm died down.
The clear morning sun began to light up
the sky. The wind suddenly stopped and
Misty tumbled back into the sea with a
splash. What a relief it was to be out of
the howling storm! As Misty plunged deep
under the waves, she wondered anxiously
where she could be. But she was certain of
one thing. She was sure that the evil

mermaid Mantora had conjured up the storm with her dark magic.

Mantora was so jealous of her sister, Queen Neptuna, that she had vowed to overthrow Coral Kingdom and set up her own Storm Kingdom in its place. She wanted to rule the seas herself as a cruel queen, helped by her army of wicked jellyfish with their poisonous stings, and

her hideous monsters from the deepest, darkest places of the ocean. Misty knew that Mantora would not want the mermaids to get the new Crystals home safely. Perhaps this storm had been part of her selfish plan to delay them in their task?

Misty steadied herself in the water with her gleaming pink tail, and looked around. A dim, early morning light made the water glow faintly. She saw that the storm had sent her to a very strange place – and she had no idea where the other mermaids were.

As Misty swam down deeper she began to see tall, dark fronds of thick seaweed growing up like trees from the sea bed.

'It doesn't look anything like Coral Kingdom,' Misty whispered. She gazed at the peculiar plants all around her and sat on a rock to think. 'This tall seaweed doesn't grow at home.'

Misty couldn't help feeling rather frightened as she started to wonder where the others could be. But just then, she noticed she was sitting on something hard and sharp.

'Ouch!' she squealed. Something had pinched her. Misty flicked her tail out of the way and peered down. A HUGE, grumpy-looking king crab was glaring up at her.

'What do you think you're doing, sitting on me like that?' the crab shouted. He snapped his big claws at Misty angrily.

'Oh...er...I'm so sorry...er...Mr Crab,' she said quickly.

'Grab?' he said. He was rather deaf. 'My name's not Grab! It's Cato. And it's not nice to be woken by a mermaid landing on your shell.'

'No, I can see that,' said Misty. 'I'm *very* sorry.'

The old crab grumbled on, but Misty was too upset to listen properly. She had to find her friends – and the way back home to Coral Kingdom – as quickly as possible. Queen Neptuna would be waiting.

'And our parents will be anxious if we are late getting home,' she thought. 'I just hope we can get back before they are too worried. But I've no idea which direction home is in! I wonder where I should look for the others? Perhaps this crab has seen them.'

The grumpy old crab was still fussing about his shell. 'There doesn't seem to be any damage done,' he was saying, 'but you must learn to look before you leap!'

'I didn't leap,' said Misty indignantly.
'I sat on you by accident.'

'Humph! I'm going back to sleep,' he
replied. 'Do NOT disturb!' He crawled
under a big frond of seaweed and
disappeared.

'Well, I don't think it will be any good
asking *him* to help find my friends,'
thought Misty. 'I'll just have to see what
I can discover for myself.'

She set off through the gently moving forest. It seemed very peaceful as Misty glided in and out of the tall strands of seaweed. Brightly coloured sea stars shone like little jewels. Sea snails crawled over the waving fronds. But there were no mermaids anywhere.

'I'll have to make the Mermaid Call,' Misty said to herself.

The Mermaid Call was very unusual and very special. It was hard to get right, but

all the Sisters of the Sea had to learn how
to make it. And if any mermaid heard a
Call, she had to answer straight away.

Misty cupped her hands around her
mouth and blew gently. A soft, echoing
noise rippled through the water. She
waited anxiously. Would any of her friends
reply, she wondered, or was she alone in
this strange place? Misty was beginning to
get really worried when, at last, a sweet
answering note floated back to her.

'That's Ellie's call!' she said. Misty
darted quickly towards the pretty sound,
then caught a glimpse of Ellie's long
brown curls and silky purple tail behind a
large seaweed-tree. Ellie didn't notice
Misty, because she was checking that her
Crystal was still safely in her pouch.

'Oh, Ellie, is it really you?' called Misty.

Ellie looked up joyfully.

'Thank goodness you're here, Misty,' she cried. 'I've been so scared! Let's try to find the others.'

Soon, the water around them echoed with their beautiful calls. One by one,

Holly, Lucy and Sophie emerged from the strange seaweed and swam towards Misty and Ellie, looking confused but relieved. They all hugged one another and smiled thankfully. But then they had serious matters to talk about.

'What do you think made the terrible storm which blew us here, Misty?' asked Lucy, with big, wondering eyes.

'I'm sure it was Mantora,' said Misty solemnly. 'She must be trying to stop us taking the Crystals home to protect Coral Kingdom. You know how she hates Queen Neptuna and wants to take over from her.'

'Yes,' agreed Holly. 'Mantora wants to ruin everything that Mother Nature made, and that Queen Neptuna protects, because she is so jealous.'

'Well, we're not going to let Mantora get away with this,' said Misty, in a determined voice. 'We're going to prove to everyone, including Mantora, that we can get those Crystals home safely. If we stick together we'll soon come up with a plan. Let's swim up to the surface. Perhaps we'll be able to work out where we are.'

'Good idea,' said Sophie. 'Let's swim as fast as we can!'

'B-but we can't,' said Lucy timidly.

'Why not?' asked Misty.

'Because of Scarlett,' Lucy replied.

Misty looked at the others with a horrified expression. They had been so worried about Mantora that they hadn't noticed that Scarlett wasn't there.

'Oh, how awful,' Misty exclaimed. 'We must find her straight away!'

Chapter Three

Misty and her friends quickly made the Mermaid Call together. But there was no reply.

'That's odd,' said Misty. 'Scarlett would call back if she could hear us.'

'Perhaps she's still in the Crystal Cave,' suggested Holly. 'She might have escaped Mantora's storm.'

'No, I don't think so, Holly,' Misty

replied. 'I heard Scarlett cry out when the storm began. She must be here too.'

'But why isn't she answering?' puzzled Ellie.

'And where *is* she?' added Sophie.

The mermaids swam slowly through the grove of seaweed, searching for their friend.

'Does anyone know what these huge plants are?' asked Misty, as she struggled though a thick, tangled patch.

'It looks like kelp,' said Holly, examining it closely with a knowledgeable air. 'I've read about this in Queen Neptuna's Sea Scrolls. And my mum sometimes uses it

in her healing potions.'

Holly's mum was a Healer back home in Coral Kingdom. Holly was very clever and loved to help her mum as she went about her important work.

'Then perhaps we're in a Giant Kelp Forest,' suggested Lucy. 'My granny told me about the Kelp Forests. She visited them when she was a young mermaid, just like us.'

'I think you're right,' agreed Holly. 'That's what it must be.'

'So who lives here?' asked Sophie. 'I hope we'll meet some dolphins!'

Sophie's special friends were the dolphins and whales and the great swimmers of the seas.

'I don't know about dolphins,' smiled

Holly, 'but the Forest will be home to many sea creatures. I saw some sea dragons and sea stars when I was looking for the rest of you.'

'And I saw all sorts of urchins and crabs and octopuses,' added Ellie.

'There might even be sea horses in a place like this,' said Lucy, with starry eyes.

'We need to find Scarlett before we can enjoy meeting the other creatures,' said Misty anxiously. 'I'm worried about her.

She must be really frightened, all on her own.'

'Poor Scarlett! I wonder where she can be,' said Ellie. 'And how can we find her?'

'It's so dark and tangled here,' replied Holly thoughtfully, 'that I think we must be in the deep heart of the Forest. Scarlett can't be near because she didn't answer our Call. Why don't we swim towards the edge of the Forest? It will be lighter there and easier to look for Scarlett.'

Misty and the others agreed that this was a good plan. The mermaids glided through the thick, tree-like stems. As they weaved their way through the dense seaweed, the paths began to get wider and it started to get lighter. They felt relieved.

Now they were sure they were getting
closer to the edge of the Forest.

'Let's make the Mermaid Call again,'
said Sophie. This time they made the notes
last longer, like sweet, clear bells. And
after a while there was a very faint reply.

'Scarlett!' said Ellie. 'Thank goodness.'

'I think she's over there,' cried Misty,
pointing at a particularly thick clump of
kelp.

They found Scarlett
looking very cross. Her
long hair had attached
itself to the branching
fronds, and she was
completely stuck.

'What are you all
staring at?' she

snapped. 'Get me out of here!'

Misty and Sophie quickly took hold of Scarlett's hands and tried to pull her free.

'OOWW!! Not like THAT!' Scarlett yelped. 'You're pulling my hair out!'

'Sorry, Scarlett,' they said. 'But how can we get you free? Your hair is tied to the kelp.'

'Perhaps I can help,' said Lucy shyly, as she rippled her emerald green tail and swam over to Scarlett. 'I've got a comb in my SOS Kit.' She opened the shiny green pouch that was tied round her waist on a little belt. Each mermaid's SOS Kit contained lots of special things. They never knew what they might need to help a sea creature in an emergency.

Lucy gently moved her Crystal to one

side and took out her Mermaid Comb. It was carved from mother-of-pearl and set with pretty green stones.

'My granny gave this to me,' she said. 'She told me it's a magic comb that never hurts. I'll try to be gentle.'

Lucy started to comb Scarlett's silky hair, carefully untangling

each strand from the seaweed. As she worked, Lucy began to sing. The others swam in a circle around Scarlett in a graceful Mermaid Dance. They all took turns to comb her hair, singing together, like a chorus of sweet sea birds:

> *Oh Mermaid, dear mermaid,*
> *You're combing your hair,*
> *Your tail is like pearl*
> *And your face is so fair!*
> *Oh Mermaid, dear mermaid,*
> *Sing your song to me,*
> *And your hair will flow free*
> *Like the beautiful Sea!*

At last, the job was done.

'I hope I didn't hurt you, Scarlett,' said Lucy.

'You all nearly pulled me to pieces,' grumbled Scarlett. She took a little mirror from her pouch and fussed over her hair.

'That's not very grateful, Scarlett,' said Sophie sharply.

'Well, let's not quarrel,' interrupted Misty. 'Queen Neptuna wouldn't want us to do that! Remember that we need to work as a team.'

Sophie and Scarlett murmured 'Sorry' to each other and Misty breathed a sigh of relief.

'Let's swim straight to the surface,' she said. 'Then we can think about how to get the Crystals home safely. We all know that some of the Merfolk thought we were too young for this task. We have to prove to them that Queen Neptuna was right to trust us.'

'I really don't think you'll be able to do that, Misty,' Scarlett said, in a rather snooty voice. All the other mermaids stared at her.

'What do you mean?' asked Ellie.

'Look!' Scarlett said, pointing dramatically. 'Misty has lost her pouch with her Crystal in it.'

Everyone gasped. Misty quickly looked down to where her pink pouch had been tied round her waist by a little sparkly belt. But the belt and the pouch had gone!

Chapter Four

'But...but...' stammered Misty, looking round wildly at her friends' puzzled faces. 'I had my pouch with me in the Crystal Cave. I remember putting my Crystal into it. I don't understand.' Misty felt so embarrassed. How could she have been so careless?

'Perhaps it fell off when we were helping Scarlett?' suggested Holly.

The mermaids started to search the grove of seaweed where Scarlett had been stuck. But suddenly Misty gasped, 'Oh dear!' Her pretty face went very white.

'What is it, Misty?' asked Ellie. 'Have you thought of something?'

'Yes,' said Misty, in a very small voice. 'Something that I was going to do, but didn't.'

'What do you mean, Misty?' said Sophie. 'You're not making sense!'

'Well,' Misty carried on, 'when I was getting ready to go to the Crystal Cave, I tied my pouch onto its belt round my waist. Then I noticed that the fastener on the belt was loose. I told myself that I should mend it straight away. But first I wanted to say goodbye to my little sister,

Dusty. And then…I'm so sorry, but I forgot to fix it.' Misty's cheeks blushed bright pink.

'Tut, tut,' said Scarlett. 'That was a big mistake, Misty! *Very* careless.'

'I know,' said Misty miserably. 'And the belt must have come undone when I crashed into the sea again, after the storm. So…'

'…So your Crystal was in your pouch,

your pouch was on the belt and the belt has fallen into the sea!' Scarlett said. 'Well, you've really let us down, Misty. What will Queen Neptuna say?'

Tears of shame filled Misty's eyes.

'Scarlett!' said Ellie reproachfully. 'Misty is very sorry. She made a mistake, but it can't be helped. It's no use rubbing it in.'

'But she'll never find her Crystal again,' said Scarlett angrily. 'It's lost in a Giant Kelp Forest! We'll never get the six new Crystals home in time now. The old Crystals will fade, our Merfolk power will die, and Mantora will destroy our home!'

Misty stopped crying and looked up. 'Oh no, she won't,' she said, in a determined voice. 'I promised Queen

Neptuna that I would bring my Crystal home safely. And I will, if it's the last thing I do!'

'We'll help you, Misty,' said Ellie eagerly. 'We're a team, after all, like you said.'

'Do you really mean it?' asked Misty.

'Of course we will,' said the others. But Scarlett still looked rather cross.

'The first thing we need is a plan,' said Holly. 'Misty, can you remember anything about where you landed after the storm?'

'Um…er…I saw lots of sea stars,' Misty said hopefully. Holly shook her head. 'That's no good,' she replied. 'There are hundreds of sea stars all over the Forest. Can't you remember anything else?'

Misty thought hard. So much seemed to have happened to her in the last two days! She desperately tried to remember what had happened when she'd arrived in the Kelp Forest. Then something flashed into her mind.

'Oh, of course! A grumpy crab pinched my tail,' she exclaimed. 'He was called…oh, what was it? "Cay" something…'

'Caleb?' suggested Ellie helpfully.

'No…wait…I know,' said Misty. 'Cato! His name was Cato!'

'Then we've got to find this Cato straight away,' said Holly. 'He's the only way we can track down the spot where the Crystal might be.'

Misty and her friends turned back the way they had come through the waving underwater thickets. They called Cato's name as they swam along.

'He was rather deaf,' said Misty. 'We'd better shout loudly.'

The mermaids' voices rang through the tall avenues of seaweed. Tiny purple fish peeped at them as they glided past. But no one answered their cries.

'Oh, this is hopeless,' said Scarlett.

'We mustn't give up yet,' said Sophie. 'Let's try just one more time. One, two, three – CAAAYY-TOW!!'

Suddenly, a giant cuttlefish poked out from behind a big piece of kelp. He waved his yellow tentacles at them.

'All right, all right!' he said. 'I heard you the first time. And the second and third...' He sounded cross, but his big eyes looked kind. 'What's the matter, mermaids?'

'We have a terrible problem...' began Misty, swimming to the front of the group

and facing the cuttlefish bravely.

'Well, there's a solution for every problem, that's my motto,' replied the cuttlefish.

'Not for this problem,' said Misty sadly. 'Unless you know someone called Cato?'

'Know him?' he said. 'Old Cato's been my special chum since we were hatched. We used to play hide and seek as youngsters in the Forest. But that was a long time ago! Now we're both sleepy old fellows.'

'That's how it all started,' said Misty. 'He was asleep and I sat on him…'

'Sat on him!' exclaimed the cuttlefish. 'That's no way to say hello to an old crab like Cato.'

'I didn't mean to,' said Misty. 'It's just that there was a terrible storm…'

'Storm? What storm? There hasn't been any storm down here in the Forest as far as I know.' The old cuttlefish looked very puzzled.

'It wasn't a storm from Mother Nature,' Misty explained. 'It was Mantora blowing us far away from our home in Coral Kingdom.'

'Mantora? Not that wicked old creature up to her tricks again. Well, well,' said the cuttlefish, eyeing the friends carefully, 'this is a strange tale. Mermaids, all the way from Coral Kingdom, unnatural storms, and now Mantora. I think you had better tell me everything that has happened from the beginning. And by the way,' he said with a smile, 'you can call me Felix.'

Chapter Five

Misty poured out the whole story to the kind old cuttlefish. As she did so, she swam restlessly backwards and forwards, to help her think better.

'So do you see, Mr Felix,' she pleaded, 'that I desperately need to find your friend Cato? I *must* ask him if he has seen my pouch with the Crystal in it.'

'Well, there's only one thing to do,' said

Felix, as he slowly unfurled his tentacles to push himself through the water. 'We must pay a visit to Cato.'

The young mermaids followed him eagerly, weaving in and out through the Forest and rippling their glistening tails. Felix puffed clumsily ahead of them. The comical cuttlefish seemed to know all the short cuts in the mysterious seaweed groves, and the mermaids started to feel a bit more hopeful. Soon, Felix nudged aside some thick strands of purple kelp. There, resting in the water, was the king crab who had pinched Misty's tail.

'Wake up, Cato old chap,' said Felix. He gently tapped the sleepy crab with his tentacles. The crab opened one eye.

'Oh, dear Mr Cato,' said Misty breathlessly, 'I really am so sorry that I woke you up by sitting on your shell. Please forgive me.'

Cato peered at Felix, and then at Misty. He seemed very confused and drowsy.

'You see, Mr Cato,' Misty explained, 'I'm in terrible trouble. I made a BIG mistake and lost my little pink pouch. That might not sound very important, but inside the pouch was a magic Crystal. And Queen Neptuna needs the Crystal to fight

Mantora and protect the sea creatures.'

'Protect the sea creatures, eh?' Cato muttered, stretching himself and waking up from his nap. 'That sounds a better idea than landing on a fellow's shell.'

'I've *got* to rescue that pink pouch,' said Misty. 'I need to know whether you saw it when I bumped into you. Did you notice it floating about after I swam away?'

'What's that?' said Cato. 'An ink couch?' He really was a bit deaf.

'No,' shouted the mermaids. 'A PINK POUCH!'

'No need to shout,' he huffed. 'Can hear perfectly well, don't you

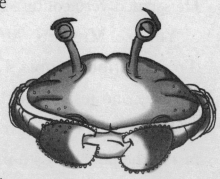

know. As a matter of fact, I did see one. Silly sort of thing, I thought. Couldn't eat it, so I gave it to some giddy little sea horses. Good day!'

Felix waved the mermaids away from the tired old crab. The purple kelp closed around Cato, and he fell back into a deep sleep.

'Now all we've got to do,' exclaimed Misty, 'is find those sea horses.'

Felix led the way towards the edge of the Forest. The kelp began to thin out. Gleaming blue and yellow fish looked up from nibbling the seaweed, wondering what six young mermaids were doing there. The sunlight shone down from the Overwater world. And at last, Misty and her friends saw the sea horses. They had curly tails and arching necks and the sweetest faces.

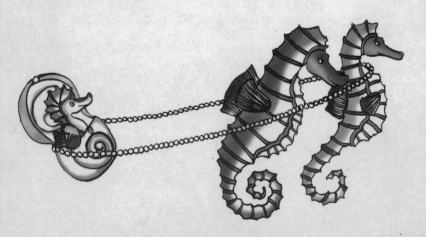

'Aren't they lovely?' breathed Lucy.

'And look,' said Misty excitedly, pointing at a father sea horse and his young family. 'They're playing with my pouch!'

The bigger sea horses were holding the ends of Misty's belt and pulling the baby along. He was sitting in the pouch as if it was a carriage, and squealing with excitement.

'He's so adorable,' said Ellie.

'Oh dear,' said Misty, in a worried voice. 'I wonder if the sea horses will be upset about giving it back? And I do hope that the Crystal hasn't fallen out to the bottom of the sea. That would be dreadful.'

There was only one way to find out...

Chapter Six

Felix told the mermaids to wait quietly while he talked to the father sea horse. Then he beckoned Misty and her friends over to be introduced.

'This is Dash the sea horse,' said Felix, 'and this is his family. I have explained why this pouch is so important to you, and to all of us sea creatures. Of course they wish to give it back to you.'

Misty took the pouch gratefully and plunged her hand in it. The Crystal was nestling safely at the bottom – and so was the golden key from the Crystal Cave. What a relief! Misty tied the broken ends of the belt firmly round her waist. She was NEVER going to make the mistake of losing her Crystal again.

'Thank you so much,' she said to Dash. 'How can I ever repay you?'

'It is an honour,' he replied, 'to help the mermaids who protect our seas.'

But Misty noticed that the baby sea horse looked very sad. He didn't understand why he couldn't play with the pouch any more.

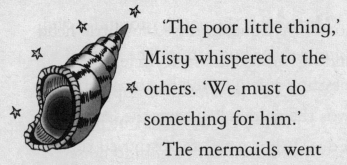

'The poor little thing,' Misty whispered to the others. 'We must do something for him.'

The mermaids went into a little huddle. Then they all smiled at the baby sea horse and said, 'Please accept these small gifts in return for Misty's pouch and Crystal.' They had all taken a trinket from their SOS Kits. There was a rattle made of bright red shells, and a piece of polished mother-of-pearl. Best of all, Misty gave him a twisty shell that blew a sweet note like a mermaid's song.

The baby, whose

name was Squeak, tossed his little head
and rushed around in a circle.

'Tank 'oo!' he squeaked happily.

The mermaids laughed. But just then,
they heard an ugly, throbbing noise
coming from the surface of the sea.

'The Cutter Boat!' cried the sea horses.
'Hide, everyone!'

They all dived down in a panic and hid
under the rocks on the sea bed.

'Follow me mermaids,' shouted Felix.
'Quickly!'

Soon Felix and the mermaids were
hiding as well. The noise grew louder.

'What's happening?' asked Misty.

'Well, mermaids,' sighed Felix, 'we have
some problems of our own here in the
Forest. My chum Cato is too old and sleepy

to notice, but things are changing round here. You see, the Humans have started to cut down the Kelp Forest.'

'Cut it down!' cried Misty. 'That's so terrible.'

'But what about all you creatures who live here?' asked Ellie. 'What will happen

to you if the Forest is destroyed?'

'We will have nowhere to live,' replied Felix sadly. 'Oh, I don't mind the Humans taking some of the kelp. They use it for food and all sorts of things. And there's plenty for everyone, if we're all sensible. But Mantora always stirs up trouble.'

'Mantora?' chorused the mermaids. 'What has she got to do with this?'

'Mantora uses her mermaid magic in bad ways,' explained Felix. 'She wants to make everything as ugly as her own dark heart, because it makes her feel more powerful. She likes to play tricks on the Humans so that they don't really think about what they do. They don't mean to be bad, but they become careless and thoughtless. So they come and chop down great chunks of the Forest, but don't give it a chance to grow back before they're after more. And that leaves us with a problem – we're in danger of losing our homes!'

'But you said that there was a solution for every problem,' said Misty.

'Not when Mantora is involved – and Humans,' said Felix. He shook his head in despair.

'But isn't there anything we can do to

rescue the Forest?' worried Misty. 'You have helped me so much, Felix, and your sea horse friends. I wish we could do something for you.'

The noise of the boat's engines throbbed above their heads. The cutting of the kelp would soon begin. The little sea horses trembled with fear.

'Think, everyone, think,' urged Sophie. The mermaids frowned with concentration. Then Misty looked up.

'I've got an idea,' she exclaimed. 'Follow me as quickly as you can.' She flicked her bright tail and sped swiftly towards the surface.

'But it will be dangerous near the boat,' protested Scarlett, darting after her. 'What are you going to do?'

'What are mermaids famous for?' called

Misty over her shoulder. 'Singing!' All the mermaids loved to sing, but Misty most of all. One day she hoped to sing for Queen Neptuna at the great Sea Festival which was held every year in Coral Kingdom. But now she was going to sing with all her strength to help her new friends.

'Of course!' said Holly. 'Mermaid singing can persuade Humans to do anything. What a brilliant idea.'

'Come on,' said Sophie, surging forward with a powerful flick of her orange tail. 'Everyone follow Misty!'

The mermaids quickly reached the surface. They could see the menacing boat, coming to cut down part of the Forest.

'We have to split up now,' Misty called

to the others. 'Then we can create a Mermaid Circle around the boat. The Circle will make our singing even more powerful. Are you ready? *Mermaid SOS!'*

'*Mermaid SOS!'* they all cried, and plunged away in different directions as fast as they could. Soon the mermaids had surrounded the boat in a wide circle. Then they started to sing:

You jolly sailors on the Sea,
Stop your work and listen to me.
You don't want to sail today,
Turn your boat and go away.
Listen to our Mermaid song,
Don't do things you know are wrong.
The Forest creatures need your help,
So don't chop down their lovely kelp!

Little by little, the boat changed its course. Then it started to head back to the distant harbour. Misty's plan had worked! The captain and crew would go home and tell a muddled story about running out of fuel, or not liking the look of the weather, and the Kelp Forest would be safe. Once the sailors had been enchanted by the Mermaid Circle of Singing, they would never be able to find that spot in the sea again.

'Hurray!' cried Misty. 'At least this time Mantora's nasty plans have been stopped. That was great singing, Scarlett.'

'Oh well,' she replied with the faintest of smiles. 'Just doing my job as part of the SOS team.'

'And you've got your Crystal back, Misty,' said Sophie happily. 'I knew you would.'

Ellie quickly squeezed Misty's hand. 'I think Queen Neptuna would be proud of you,' she said.

'Well, I did manage to put my mistake right,' said Misty, with a relieved grin.

'*And* rescue the Forest,' said Holly.

'We all did that,' said Misty. 'We really are a team. Let's go back and tell everyone

that they're safe now.' The mermaids all dived in an arc like a rainbow, speeding down through the water to their friends.

The sea creatures were so happy when they heard the good news. The sea dragons and octopuses and spiny urchins who lived in the Forest came to thank the mermaids.

Squeak kissed them with tiny baby kisses.
But Cato was still fast asleep…

It was time for Misty and her friends to
set off on their journey home. Queen
Neptuna would be waiting anxiously for
them – and for their magic Crystals.

'Mantora's storm sent you far from Coral
Kingdom,' said Felix. 'We will guide you
out of the Forest and on your way. Then
you need to travel to the West. Always
follow the setting sun, but look out for
Mantora. You never know when she might
strike again. Be careful, brave mermaids.'

'Be car'foo!' said Squeak.

'We will!' replied the mermaids. They
swam with their friends through the last
rows of purple kelp, until they saw the
open sea ahead. Looking over their

shoulders, they had one final glimpse of
the dark, mysterious Forest, its seaweed
trees swaying gently in the water. The
mermaids were so happy that they had
been able to save it from destruction.

'Goodbye, Dash,' they called. 'Goodbye,
little Squeak. And goodbye, dear Felix.
We'll never forget you.'

Misty and her friends held up their
glittering Crystals in farewell, showering
sparks of light all around them. Then they

put the precious Crystals away carefully
and set out for Coral Kingdom.

What would happen to the mermaids on
the next part of their journey? And would
they get home in time with the Crystals?

Mermaid Sisters of the Sea

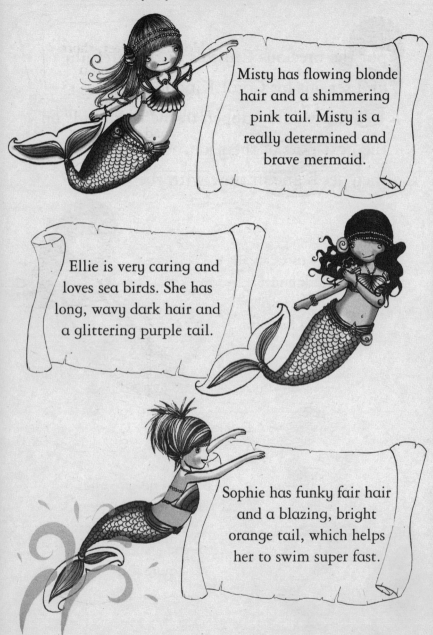

Misty has flowing blonde hair and a shimmering pink tail. Misty is a really determined and brave mermaid.

Ellie is very caring and loves sea birds. She has long, wavy dark hair and a glittering purple tail.

Sophie has funky fair hair and a blazing, bright orange tail, which helps her to swim super fast.

Holly has sweet, short black hair and a dazzling yellow tail. Holly is very thoughtful and clever.

Scarlett has fabulous, thick dark hair and a gleaming red tail. She can be a little bit bossy and headstrong sometimes.

Lucy has fiery red hair and an emerald green tail, but don't let that fool you – she is really quite shy.

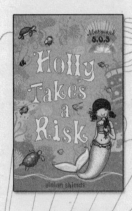